To Sheri—it still is and always will be yours.
—J.F.

For Garcelle, Sonriza, Howard, and Lidia.
Thanks for the exposure to Dutch love, fun, and culture.
See you in Amsterdam.
—"Christie"

Text copyright © 2003 by Jeron Ashford Frame
Illustrations copyright © 2003 by R. Gregory Christie

Tricycle Press
a little division of Ten Speed Press
P.O. Box 7123
Berkeley, California 94707
www.tenspeed.com

Design by Betsy Stromberg
Typeset in Spleeny Decaf
The illustrations in this book were rendered in acrylic and gouache.

Library of Congress Cataloging-in-Publication Data

Frame, Jeron Ashford.
 Yesterday I had the blues / by Jeron Ashford Frame ; illustrations by
R. Gregory Christie.
    p. cm.
Summary: A young boy ponders a variety of emotions and how different
members of his family experience them, from his own blues to his
father's grays and his grandmother's yellows.
 ISBN 1-58246-084-1
 [1. Emotions--Fiction. 2. Family life--Fiction. 3. African
Americans--Fiction.] I. Christie, Gregory, 1971-, ill. II. Title.
 PZ7.F8445 Ye 2003
 [E]--dc21

                    2002155295

First Tricycle Press printing, 2003
Printed in China

2 3 4 5 6 7 — 08 07 06 05 04

Yesterday I Had the BLUES

by Jeron Ashford Frame

Illustrations by R. Gregory Christie

TRICYCLE PRESS
Berkeley/Toronto

Yesterday I had the
blues.

Not the rain on the sidewalk blues,
or the broken skateboard blues, or the
outgrew my favorite football jersey blues.

Not even the Monday mornin'
cold cereal instead of pancakes blues.

Uh-uh,

I had those deep down in my shoes blues,
the go away, Mr. Sun, quit smilin' at me blues.

The hold a pillow,
wish it was tomorrow blues.

The kind of blues
make you wanna just

turn

down

the

volume.

But today I got the
greens.

The runnin' my hand along the hedges greens.

The down to the drugstore
and beyond,
dirt in my socks
greens.

The kind of
greens make you
want to be Somebody.

Daddy says he got the
grays.

The straight
shoelaces,
coffee in the car
grays.

The lines
between his eyes,
lookin' at his watch
grays.

FINE
$50

The don't ask for a new skateboard till tomorrow grays.

Poor Daddy.

NO PARKING

FROM

Sasha says she got the
pinks.

The shiny tights,
ballet after school,
glitter on her cheeks pinks.

The where's my butterfly
hair clip? pinks.

The kind of pinks
make me
want to catch the next bus.

Talia says she got the
indigos.

I said, indigo's the same as blue.

Talia says, uh-uh,
she got the saxophone
in the subway
indigos.

The hair hangin' loose,
write a poem that don't rhyme indigos.

The kind of indigos
make her act
like the drapes.

Gram's got the
yellows,
I can tell.

The hummin' that parade song,
flower house slipper yellows.

The mix up some
oatmeal raisin cookies
                              (I hope)
yellows.

Mama
says
she
got
the
reds.

Look out!

Yeah, yesterday I had the
blues.

Today I got the
greens.

Tomorrow maybe it'll be the
silvers.

The rocket-powered skateboard silvers!

And around here, that's okay.
'Cause together we got somethin'
that'll never change.

We got a family—
the kind of family makes you feel
like it's

all

golden.